*For Tiziana*

J. 42,934
£7.99

First published 1993 by Walker Books Ltd
87 Vauxhall Walk, London SE11 5HJ

Text © 1993 Martin Waddell
Illustrations © 1993 John Bendall-Brunello

Printed and bound in Italy by
LEGO, Vicenza

British Library Cataloguing in Publication Data
A catalogue record for this book is available
from the British Library.

ISBN 0-7445-2278-1

# THE BIG BAD MOLE'S COMING!

Written by
**MARTIN WADDELL**

Illustrated by
**JOHN BENDALL~BRUNELLO**

WALKER BOOKS
LONDON

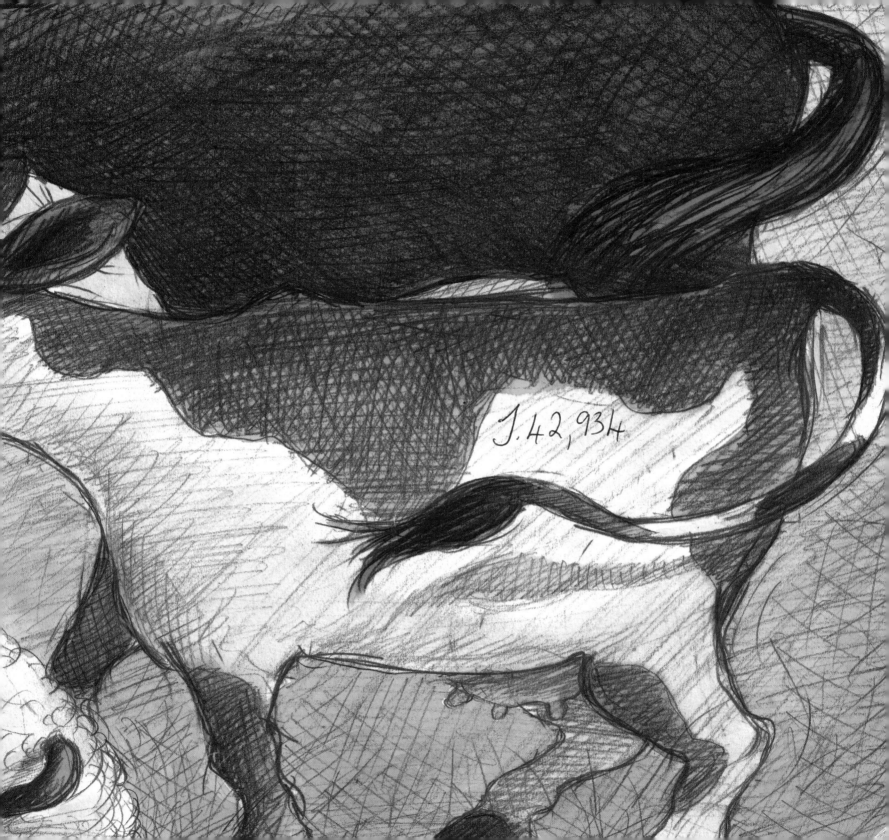